"Let's take a shortcut through Johnson's Woods," suggested Chip.

"But my mom told us not to go in there after dark."

"It's not dark yet," he pointed out. "But we'll have to hurry."

"I don't know." The wooded path looked like a giant tongue leading into a black, endless mouth. I rubbed the goosebumps prickling my arm. "It looks creepy in there."

"Rule Number One," recited Daphne. "Ghouls are scary, but never scared."

"Oh, that's right." I took a deep breath. "Okay. Let's go!"

THE Ghoul Brothers

THE Ghoul Brothers

by Lee Wardlaw
illustrated by Brian Floca

Troll

For Sherry Shahan:
A good friend
and a very nice ghoul!

Text copyright © 1996 by Lee Wardlaw Jaffurs.
Illustrations copyright © 1996 by Troll Communications L.L.C.

Published by Troll Communications L.L.C.

Printed in the United States of America.

10 9 8 7 6 5 4 3 2 1

Table of Contents

1
A Scary Invitation

"Hey, Nick! Wait up!"

I skidded to a stop and glanced back at our fourth grade classroom.

Big mistake.

Heather Hancock waved, her hand flapping like bat wings. Then she squeezed through a knot of kids. School had ended for the day, and everyone was trying to cram through the door at the same time.

My best friend Chip and I sit in the last row, but we're always the first kids into the hall. That's because we take a secret shortcut. (Behind the aquarium, through the coat room, and *under* our teacher's desk.)

"Wait up!" Heather flapped again. She skirted toward us.

"Quick!" I said to Chip. "Hide me!"

Maybe I could duck into the boys' room. Or

crawl inside a drinking fountain. Or . . .

Too late. Heather grabbed my sleeve.

"*Hi*," she said, wiggling her nose like a bunny. She'd been doing that for eight months. Ever since Valentine's Day. The day I got my envelopes mixed up.

My ears itched just thinking about it.

I'd bought a special valentine for my favorite teacher, Ms. Cook. It had a cartoon of a walrus sitting on an iceberg. He was hugging a big pink heart in his flippers. The card said: *I'll Walrus Love You.*

"I'll walrus love you, too," Heather whispered in my ear while serving the party cupcakes.

That's when I knew.

I had accidentally given *Heather* Ms. Cook's card!

"We'll miss the bus," Chip complained. He shifted his bookpack from one shoulder to the other.

"This won't take long," Heather said.

She looked to the left. To the right. Then, in a mysterious voice, she singsonged: "Hold out your hands and close your eyes, and you will get a *scary* surprise."

A Halloween skeleton hanging on the wall gave me a toothy grin.

"Um, is it a monster?" I asked.

"No," said Heather.

"Is it homework?" Chip asked.

"No!" said Heather.

"Is it . . ." I gulped ". . . a love letter?"

"*NO!*" Heather stomped her foot.

"We give up," Chip said with a shrug. "Those are the scariest things we know."

Heather made a face. "Just hold out your hands!"

"Oh, all right," I agreed.

"And close your eyes."

"They're closed."

"And no peeking!"

"Okay, okay!"

Heather set something in my hand. It felt like an envelope. Oh, no. Maybe it *was* a love letter!

"You can open your eyes now," Heather said, wiggling her nose. "Oh, yeah. Here's one for you, too, Chip," she added. Then she raced down the hall, her black hair streaming behind her like Dracula's cape.

I stared at the envelope. My name was penciled on the front in Heather's loopy handwriting. She'd dotted the *i* with a tiny heart.

Chip elbowed me in the ribs. "C'mon, the bus is here!"

We thundered out to the parking lot. I shivered as the October wind tickled through my jacket like cold, bony fingers.

Only one seat left. We thumped into it just as the bus groaned to a start.

"So what is it?" Chip asked, flicking the envelope.

"I don't know." I held it at arm's length like it might be a vampire ready to bite me.

"Unless you have X-ray vision," Chip said, "you'll have to open it."

"No way. *You* open *yours*."

"Uh-uh. *You* got *yours* first."

I took a deep breath. "Okay. Here goes . . ."

I ripped the seal.

Out fluttered a handmade invitation. It was cut in the shape of a bat, and had a picture of a witch with a green face and warts. She was flying on a broomstick. The invitation said:

❧   ❧   ❧

Please Come to My Halloween Party!
When: The spookiest, scariest night of the year
Time: The Witching Hour (four o'clock)
Where: Heather's Haunted House
Tricks! Treats! Games! Prizes!
Grand Prize for the spookiest, scariest costume!

"Cool!" said Chip. "Want to go?"

"I don't know. What if Heather tries to . . . *kiss* me?"

"I won't let her."

"How will you stop her?" I asked.

Chip squinted, thinking. Then he grinned. "I'll *breathe* on her," he said.

My best friend has notorious potato chip breath. That's because potato chips are his favorite food. He sprinkles them on cereal. He spreads them in peanut butter sandwiches. He mashes them into mashed potatoes and gravy.

I'll bet he even crumbles them in ice cream.

Which is why everyone calls him Chip. (Nobody but me remembers his real name is Jose.)

I'm glad I don't eat *my* favorite food all day. Or else, everyone would call me Spaghetti.

"This sour cream-and-chive flavor should do the trick," Chip said, pulling a snack-sized bag from his pack. "They're my Secret Weapon. Here, let me demonstrate." He munched a handful. The onion fumes almost knocked me over.

"Perfect," I said, edging closer to the window. I zipped my jacket over my nose. "But you know how Heather likes to follow me around. You'll have to stick by my side the whole party."

"I will." *Crunch, crunch*.

"Promise?"

"Sure." *Nibble, crunch*.

"Even in the bathroom?"

Chip froze in mid-munch. "Yes," he said at last.

"Cross your heart?"

He did. It left a greasy X stain on the front of his jacket.

"Okay. If *you'll* go to the party, *I'll* go to the party."

"And *I'll* go if *you'll* go."

"It's settled then," I said. "We'll go."

"Good." Chip poured the last crumbs into his mouth, licked his fingers, then wadded the empty bag into his pack. "I—" he announced "—want to win the Grand Prize."

"Me, too!" I said. "What are you going to be?"

Chip looked behind him to make sure no one was listening. "I don't know," he admitted in a whisper. "Something spooky. What are you going to be?"

"I don't know. Something scary. Maybe if I look *really* scary, Heather will be afraid to kiss me."

Chip laughed. "Let's think of a costume together. My dad always says, "Two heads are better than one."

I snapped my fingers. "That gives me a great idea!"

2
Meet the Ghoul Brothers

On Halloween, Chip and I went to my house after school to get dressed for the party.

"Do you want a snack?" I asked, plucking an apple from the fruit bowl.

"Nah," Chip said. "I brought my own." He pulled a bag of barbecued you-know-whats from his jacket pocket and started munching.

"What about the Secret Weapon?"

From his other pocket, Chip pulled the sour cream-and-chive bag. "I'm saving the Secret Weapon for later," he said.

"Good thinking. C'mon, let's get ready."

We locked ourselves in the bathroom to do our make-up and costume.

Half an hour later, Chip wore a crumpled hat, sunglasses, and an oozing gash on his forehead.

I wore a pirate patch over one eye, a ratty wig, and a ragged scar on my cheek.

Next, we struggled into a big wool coat I'd borrowed from Dad. Chip put on the left sleeve, and I put on the right. Then we squished together and buttoned the coat up the front.

We admired ourselves in the mirror.

"We look spooky," Chip said.

"Scary," I agreed.

"Um, what are we again?" he asked.

"A two-headed ghoul."

"Oh, yeah. That's right." Chip bit into a chip. "Um, what's a ghoul?"

"Well, it's a . . . sort of um . . . kind of like . . ." I cleared my throat. "I can't remember *exactly*. Let's look it up."

Dad's coat reached to our ankles, so we had to shuffle to my bedroom.

I opened the dictionary. "Ghost . . . ghost town . . . ghost writer . . . here it is! Ghoul." I read aloud: *"An evil spirit that robs graves and feeds on the flesh of the dead."*

My stomach flipped a somersault.

Chip's face turned green under his gash.

"Gross," he said.

"Maybe we could be vegetarian ghouls," I suggested.

Chip nodded and crunched. "If *you* won't tell,

I won't tell."

"And *I* won't, if *you* won't."

"It's settled then. We won't tell." He munched a last mouthful, breathing smoky fumes into my face. "Ready to go?"

I coughed. "Um, would you mind gargling first?"

"Sure."

We shuffled back into the bathroom. I took a bottle of mint mouthwash from the cupboard.

"Is that better?" he asked, smacking his lips.

"Much," I lied. Now his breath smelled like barbecued toothpaste.

"Hey, let's scare your mom!" Chip said.

"Yeah!"

We sneaked up behind her in the den. *"WOO-HOOO-AHH-HA-HA!"* we laughed in our scary laugh.

"Goodness!" Mom cried. She clutched at her chest, faking a heart attack. "What are *you*?"

"Not what," I said. "Who. We are the Ghoul Brothers, at your service." We bowed. "This is Chip Ghoul."

Chip sneered.

"And I am Nicholas H. Ghoul."

I snarled.

"What does the 'H' stand for?" Mom asked.

"Hairy."

"Yes, you certainly are."

"How do I look?" asked Chip.

"Awful," Mom said.

"How do *I* look?" I asked.

"Awful," she repeated.

Chip and I slapped a High Five. "The Grand Prize is ours!" I cheered. "Let's trick-or-treat on the way to the party. I bet we can scare a lot of people."

"Wait! Let me take your picture." Mom rummaged through her desk till she found the camera. "Smile!"

"The Ghoul Brothers never smile," I said.

"But we do have our scary laugh," said Chip.

"WOO-HOOO-AHH-HA-HA!"

Mom snapped the picture.

We shuffled toward the door.

"Let's double-check that we have everything," I said. "Extra make-up?"

"Check."

"Treat bags?"

"Check."

"Secret Weapon?"

Chip patted his pocket and grinned a ghoulish grin. "Check."

"Be home before seven," Mom called after us.

"We will."

"Don't go into Johnson's Woods after dark."

"We won't."

"Don't forget your sister."

Chip and I froze.

"Sister?" I asked, pretending to act surprised. "The Ghoul Brothers don't have a sister. You must have mistaken us for the Goblin Brothers."

Mom didn't hear. "Daphne!" she called. "The boys are ready to go!"

My little sister tippy-toed out of her bedroom. She was dressed as a butterfly. She wore a froo-froo skirt and frilly wings. Two feelers on her head bobbed with every step. *Boing-Boing*.

Chip moaned.

I groaned.

"The Ghoul Brothers can't trick-or-treat with a butterfly," I said in horror. "We have our scary reputations to protect."

"If you don't take Daphne with you," Mom warned, "you'll spend the night protecting that reputation in your room."

Chip and I looked at each other and sighed.

"Goodbye!" we said, and tugged Daphne out the door.

3
Trick-or-Treat!

Dry leaves skipped across the sidewalk. A jack-o'-lantern winked from the porch of the first house.

Daphne hid her face in our coat.

"It's *easy*," I explained. "Just go up the steps and ring the bell. Then shout trick-or-treat!"

"Come *with* me." Daphne clutched my hand.

"We'll follow behind you," I said. "Ghouls aren't allowed to trick-or-treat with butterflies."

"Why not?"

"Um, well, *because*," I answered.

"Can *I* be a ghoul?" Daphne asked.

"Sure," Chip said. "If you promise to obey the Ghoul Rules. Rule Number One: Ghouls are scary, but never scared."

Daphne gulped.

"Rule Number Two," I said. "Ghouls never smile. They only laugh a scary laugh. *WOO-*

25

HOOO-AHH-HA-HA!"

Daphne shivered.

"Rule Number Three." Chip peered at her over the top of his sunglasses. "Ghouls only eat lizard pancakes."

"Ewww!" Daphne cried. She scampered up the steps and rang the bell.

"Don't you want to hear Rule Number Four?" Chip called.

The door opened. A grandma-looking lady came out.

"Trick-or-treat!" my sister said with a curtsy. Her feelers went *Boing-Boing*.

"Oh, aren't you *precious*!" the lady cooed. She dropped a candy bar into Daphne's bag.

"And look at those *darling* feelers!"

Two more candy bars dropped in.

"And where did you get those *beautiful* wings?"

Three more candy bars.

And a Tootsie Pop.

And bubble gum.

I gave a low whistle. "Wow!"

"Eureka!" Chip crowed. "We've struck gold. Let's go!"

We shuffled to the door as fast as we could, and held out our bags.

Chip growled.

I snarled.

"Oh, my," the lady said, her smile fading. "Who—who are you?"

We bowed.

"Ghoul is the name," I announced, "and scaring is our game."

"Well, how nice." Something went *thump* into each of our bags.

The lady smiled again. At my *sister.* "Good-bye, honey. You are so pretty. Happy Halloween!"

She shut the door.

"No fair," I grumbled. "Daphne got more stuff than we did!"

Chip shook his head sadly. "Not one single potato chip."

"Well, all I got was this measly stick of gum." I bit into it. "And it's *stale*!" I stared at Daphne, making my eyes real big and pleading, just like Buddy's, her stuffed bear. "Wouldn't you like to share?" I begged in my best stuffed-bear voice.

"But ghouls only eat lizard pancakes," Daphne reminded.

"And candy bars," I said. "For dessert."

"And sometimes," added my friend, "a potato chip or two. For medicinal purposes, of course."

"Oh." Daphne dug in her bag and pulled out two candy bars.

"You know," said Chip, chomping into one, "there are times when ghouls must bend their rules."

"You're absolutely right," I agreed. "Sometimes butterflies need our help."

I took Daphne's hand. We marched together to the next house and rang the bell.

The door opened.

"Trick-or-treat!"

"Well, aren't you a pretty one!" said a man as he gazed at Daphne. He chuckled the way Santa Claus does when you're sitting on his lap at the mall, telling him your Christmas list.

He chuckled again and scratched his bald head. "Tell me, what are you, sweetheart?"

"I'm a ghoul!"

"Yes, I know you're a girl."

"She's a butterfly," I put in. "And we're her brother."

"You do look alike." The man dropped three candy bars into Daphne's bag. Then he gave Chip and me three candy bars, too.

"Thank-you!" chirped Daphne, as the door shut.

"Rule Number Four," I said. "Ghouls never say thank-you. It ruins their scary reputation."

Daphne nodded, and we hurried to the next house.

And the next house.

And the next.

After an hour, our bags were so heavy my arm ached.

"Look at all this loot!" Chip cried, gawking into his sack.

"Let's go to Heather's party now," I said, "before—" I stopped.

I looked to the left. To the right. "Before the Pumpkin Smasher sees us," I whispered.

"Who's the Pun-kin Smasher?" Daphne asked.

"He's one mean guy," said Chip. "He's a seventh grader with rub-on tattoos. *Snake* tattoos. And he steals people's jack-o'-lanterns and smashes them in the street. *Splat-Splat.*"

"He steals bags of candy, too," I said. "His favorite trick is to steal them from butterflies."

Daphne hugged her bag.

"But have no fear. The Ghoul Brothers are here. Hey, Chip, isn't it time to employ the S.W.?"

"S.W.?" He looked confused. "What's that?"

"*You* know. The Secret Weapon!"

"Oh, yeah. Right." He eased the bag from his pocket and ripped it open with his teeth. Quickly, he poured a stream of chips into his mouth.

The air smelled like woodsmoke, pumpkin pie, . . . and chopped onions.

Big ones.

Tears pricked my eyes.

"P.U.," Daphne said, pinching her nose.

"Rule Number Five," Chip crunched. "Ghouls must have bad breath at all times."

I heard a rustling behind me and peeked over my shoulder.

Had that shadow moved?

I shuddered. "Come on!" I said. "Let's hurry!"

4
Heather's Haunted House

Heather lived in a big farmhouse on the edge of Johnson's Woods. The trees creaked and groaned, shrieked and moaned in the wind.

Daphne tried to crawl underneath our coat.

"Spooky," said Chip.

"Scary," I agreed.

We knocked on Heather's door.

A green witch with a pointed black hat and warts let us in. She wiggled her nose at me. A wart on the end of it danced around.

"*Hi,* Nick," the witch said.

I looked down and scuffed my sneakers. "Hi, Heather," I mumbled.

She sounded disappointed. "How'd you know it was me?"

Ha! I would have known that wiggly bunny nose anywhere. "Um," I began, "I recognized your—" I started to say "warts," but changed it to "voice."

"Really?" Heather's nose zoomed into wiggling warp-speed. She sidled closer.

I nudged Chip inside the coat. Secret Weapon time.

"HHHI, HHHEATHER," he said. A hurricane of onion breath gusted out of his mouth.

Heather blinked a few times and took a step backward. She put a hand over her nose.

"Something wrong?" I asked.

"Oh, uh, no. My nose is just cold. So what are you guys supposed to be?"

"We're the Ghoul Brothers. Ghoul is our name and scaring is our game."

"HHHAVEN'T you HHHEARD of us?" Chip asked with gale-force onions.

Heather could only shake her head.

"Shall we demonstrate our scary laugh?" he asked.

"We shall," I answered. *"WOO-HOOO-AHH-HA-HA!"*

Heather squealed. "Oooh, you guys are scary!"

I winked at Chip. The Grand Prize was ours for sure.

"Hey, who's this?" Heather asked.

Daphne had crawled out from under our coat. I rolled my eyes. "My sister. Sorry. Mom made me bring her."

"That's okay," Heather said. "My little sister is here, too. C'mon."

She led us downstairs.

The basement was lit with creepy orange lights. Fake spiderwebs hung from the ceiling. A bubbling cauldron squatted in one corner. Our whole class was there. Goblins and ghosts. Monsters and cats. Creatures and werewolves and bats.

We ate popcorn balls, and pumpkin cakes with candy corn eyes. We drank a fizzy witches' brew and listened to a creepy tape of rattling chains and howling dogs.

Heather followed us around for a while. But every time she got too close, Chip would attack with another blast of the Secret Weapon.

"HHHAPPY HHHALLOWEEN, HHHEATHER," he said.

Heather backed off with a sigh.

"Time for the games!" she announced.

"Keep your eye on us," I said to Daphne. "Ghouls are very good at games."

"And they always win prizes," Chip agreed.

"Let's start with Pin the Fang on the Vampire," Heather suggested. She held up a scarf. "Who wants to go first?" She gazed at me and wiggled her nose.

"We have to go to the bathroom," I said.

36

Heather tied the blindfold on Gary, instead. He had masking tape wrapped around his body, and Band-Aids stuck to his face. I think he was supposed to be a mummy.

"Careful!" Gary fussed. "The blindfold is squishing my Band-Aids! I paid four dollars and sixty-nine cents a box for those."

"Just don't peek," Heather said. She twirled him three times.

He rocked.

He swayed.

Then he staggered toward a picture of a vampire taped on the wall. He pinned the fang on the vampire's knee.

We all cracked up.

"Next!" Heather said, waving the scarf.

"Me, me, me, me, me!" cried Maria, a lady Frankenstein in fishing waders. She thunked and clunked around blindfolded, finally pinning the fang on the edge of his cape.

We cracked up again.

Other kids took their turns. The vampire grew fangs on his foot, stomach, and eyebrow.

Then it was the Ghoul Brothers' turn.

"You could save time and give us the prize now," I said.

Heather just giggled and handed us each a fang.

"HHHEATHER, do you need HHHELP with that HHHANDKERCHIEF?" Chip asked.

Heather coughed and tied the scarf over his eyes at arm's length. Then she tied another blind-fold on me.

"Good luck!" she whispered in my ear.

She shoved us around in a circle once, twice, three times.

We stomped on each other's feet and were so dizzy we almost fell over.

"Ouch! This way," said Chip.

"Ow! No, that-a-way," I said.

Chip went his way.

I went on mine.

Bonk-Bonk.

We bounced into each other inside the coat.

"Quit it!" said Chip.

"*You* quit it," I cried.

We staggered forward a few steps. At last, we pinned our fangs on the vampire. But when we took off our blindfolds, we saw it was a lamp. A lamp across the room!

Everyone cracked up even harder than before. This time I didn't think it was very funny.

"Can I try?" asked Daphne.

I snorted.

Heather said, "Sure!" She moved the vampire lower on the wall. Then she blindfolded Daphne, twirled her, and gave a little push.

Daphne wobbled forward on twinkle toes, her feelers going *Boing-Boing.* She pinned the fang on the vampire's nose.

Chip and I laughed so hard we almost fell over.

"Daphne is the closest!" Heather exclaimed. "She wins!"

"What?!" I said.

"Huh?!" said Chip.

Everyone clapped.

"How did she *do* that?" my friend grumbled.

"Maybe she peeked," I growled.

Heather gave Daphne a surprise bag. Inside was a rubber tarantula on a string. The tarantula had hairy legs and red eyes.

"Wow!" I muttered.

"Cool!" Chip murmured.

Daphne scampered over to us. "Look what I got!" she said. "Do you want to play with it?"

"No," I said, faking a yawn. "Ghouls only play with *real* tarantulas. *Poisonous* tarantulas."

"Besides," added Chip, "Nick and I will win a

tarantula in the next game. Just wait and see. Right, Nick?"

"Right." We slapped a High Five. "Because Ghoul is our name and winning is our game!"

5
And the Winner Is . . .

"Time to bob for apples!" Heather said. "Who wants to go first?"

"Yuk-yuk, not me!" laughed T.J. "My clown wig would get wet." He danced a quick jig in floppy shoes as long as submarine sandwiches. "I'd love to let my hair down, but that would be a hair-brained scheme, with hair-raising results! Yuk-yuk! And you know the old saying, 'Hair today, gone tomorrow!'"

"Uh-huh," said Heather. "What about you, Sherry?"

"It-would-not-be-ad-vis-a-ble-for-me-to-vol-un-teer," Sherry answered in a flat, mechanical voice. She was dressed as a robot with blinking calculators attached to her silver leotard. "The-wa-ter-could-o-ver-load-my-cir-cui-try. I-would-be-forced-to-self-de-struct. Beep!"

"What a bunch of wimps!" Chip muttered.

"We'll show 'em." I raised my voice over the party chatter. "The Ghoul Brothers aren't scared of a little water," I declared. "Stand aside!"

Chip and I pushed through the crowd. We leaned over a tub of floating apples.

"Here's the plan," I said. "I'll push an apple toward you with my nose. Then, you bite it."

"No noses allowed," warned Heather in a bossy voice. "Only lips and teeth."

"How about this," Chip offered. "I'll push an apple to the bottom of the tub with my lips. I'll bite it from there. Ready?"

"Wait—are you crazy?" I demanded. "You'll drown me!"

But Chip didn't hear. He ducked his head into the water, dragging me with him.

The water was cold. Iceberg cold. I held my breath as long as I could. Then I yanked us up, sputtering and coughing.

"Hey!" Chip hollered. Water dripped off his sunglasses. "I almost had it! Let me try again."

"Forget it," I grumbled. Cold water ran down my neck, under the collar of Dad's coat. The wool started to smell like a wet cat. A wet cat with sour cream-and-chive breath.

Heather handed us each a towel. "Better luck

next time," she singsonged, wiggling her warty nose. "Anyone else want to try?"

No one did.

"I will," piped a small voice.

Before the Ghoul Brothers could stop her, Daphne tippy-toed up to the tub and splashed in, face first.

"Save her!" I cried. "She can't swim!"

"Help!" Heather yelled. "Mom, Dad, come quick!"

"They're upstairs! Somebody call 9-1-1!"

I had to do something. *Fast.*

I dragged Chip forward. Plunged my arm into the icy water. Yanked Daphne out by her wings.

She hiccuped. Water streamed off her, making a puddle on the floor. Her feelers were soggy. Instead of going *Boing-Boing,* they went *Slog-Slog.* She looked like the wet cat I'd smelled. But she had a tiny apple clenched in her teeth.

"Hurray!" Heather cheered. "Daphne wins again!"

"What?!" I said.

"Huh?!" said Chip.

Heather's mom ran into the room. When she saw Daphne, she made a funny sound in her throat. She fussed and fretted, and rubbed Daphne

with two fluffy towels. Then Heather gave my sister a surprise bag. This one was long and slim. Inside was a magic wand.

"Look what I got!" Daphne proudly clutched the wand in her fingers. "Can this turn me into a ghoul?"

"That's not a *real* magic wand," I said, with another fake yawn. "It's only a stick, painted with glitter."

"Oh." Daphne held out her apple. "Want a bite?"

"No, thank you," I said. "Rule Number Three: Ghouls only eat candy bars and lizard pancakes."

"Oh, yeah." Daphne gave her apple to Sherry.

"And now," said Heather, "the moment you've all been waiting for! My mom and dad will choose the spookiest, scariest costume. The winner will receive . . . the Grand Prize!" She gazed at me, her bunny nose wiggling double-time.

Chip and I winked at each other.

Heather's dad cleared his throat. "Judging this contest was tough. We've seen a lot of fine costumes here tonight. But we've finally reached a unanimous decision . . ."

Chip and I nudged each other.

"And the winner is . . ."

I held my breath.

"The winner is . . . Gary the Mummy!"

"What?!" I said.

"Huh?!" said Chip.

Everyone clapped and whistled and cheered.

Heather gave Gary a giant, bulging bag. The Grand Prize. The best prize of all.

The prize that should've been ours.

"Congratulations, Gary!" Heather shouted. She snatched off her witch hat and waved it in the air. And then she did something surprising.

She wiggled her nose at him.

Hmmm. Maybe losing wasn't so bad, after all.

"Should I tell Gary about the Secret Weapon?" Chip murmured in my ear.

I shook my head. I didn't think he'd need it. Because Gary was wiggling his nose back at Heather!

Daphne started to cry. "I wanted the Ghoul Brothers to win!" she wailed.

The crowd turned to stare at us.

"Rule Number Five," I whispered in her ear. "Ghouls are very brave, even when they lose. They dry their tears and say, 'Maybe next year.'"

"Oh," said Daphne. "Maybe next year." She sniffed and wiped her eyes.

"Let's go home," I said.

"Good-bye, Heather! Thank you, Heather!" we called. "Happy Halloween!"

Heather waved. Then she went back to wiggling her nose at Gary.

We shuffled outside. The sky was turning purple.

"It's late," I said. "My mom will be mad."

"Let's take a shortcut through Johnson's Woods," suggested Chip.

"But my mom told us not to go in there after dark."

"It's not dark yet," he pointed out. "But we'll have to hurry."

"I don't know." The wooded path looked like a giant tongue leading into a black, endless mouth. I rubbed the goosebumps prickling my arm. "It looks creepy in there."

"Rule Number One," recited Daphne. "Ghouls are scary, but never scared."

"Oh, that's right." I took a deep breath. "Okay. Let's go!"

6
The Pumpkin Smasher

"It's—it's dark in here," stammered Chip. He gulped. "Where's the flashlight?"

"*I* don't have it," I said. "I thought *you* had it."

"No, *I* don't have it. I thought *you* had it!"

"It's settled then," I said. "We don't have it."

A dog howled.

A branch cracked.

Had that shadow moved?

"Oh-oh," said Chip.

I felt creepy-crawlies skip down my neck. I squeezed Daphne's hand. "Let's walk faster," I said.

The shadow moved again. It stepped in front of us, blocking our path. "What's your hurry?" it demanded.

Then I saw its face. And tattoos.

Snake tattoos.

The Pumpkin Smasher!

"Run!" I shouted.

"This way," yelled Chip.

"No, that-a-way," I cried.

Chip went his way. Daphne and I went mine. *Bonk-Bonk.* We bounced into each other, then fell in a heap on the ground.

The Smasher stood over us. "Gimme your bag," he ordered with a sneer. He grabbed it from Chip's hands.

"Quick!" Daphne whispered. "Laugh your scary laugh."

I opened my mouth. But all that came out was: "woo-hoo-hee-hee-hee."

"Did someone sneeze?" asked the Smasher.

"Oh, yes, so sorry," I said.

"Give me *your* bag," the Smasher growled. He tore it from my hands.

"Quick!" Daphne whispered. "Tell him about the lizard pancakes."

"Another time," I squeaked.

The Smasher looked at Daphne.

"I'll bet *you* have the most candy." He laughed an evil laugh and reached for her bag. Daphne's lips quivered.

"Leave her alone!" I shouted.

I leaped up, dragging Chip with me.

"You've got our candy," I said. "You don't need hers, too. So go away."

"Make me!" the Smasher taunted.

My hands turned into fists. I stepped toward him.

"Excuse me, Mr. Smasher," said Daphne. "But there's a spider on your foot."

"Oh, yeah? Where?" The Smasher looked down. A big tarantula with hairy legs and red eyes sat on his shoe. It started to jerk up his leg.

"AAAARRRGGHHH!" screamed the Smasher.

He dropped the bags of candy and ran away.

"What?!" I said.

"Huh?!" said Chip.

Daphne held up a piece of string. A tarantula dangled from the end of it.

Chip and I laughed.

"I forgot all about your prize," Chip admitted. "C'mon, let's get out of here before the Smasher comes back!"

We scuttled along the path. Burst through the trees. We didn't stop until we saw the friendly, yellow glow of the porch light at my house just ahead.

Then we pulled Daphne into a hug.

"Thank-you for saving us," I said.

"Ghouls never say thank-you," she reminded us.

I hugged her again. "There are times when even ghouls must bend their rules."

"Speaking of ghouls," Chip said, "don't you think Daphne would make a good one?"

"I don't know." I looked her over from the top of her feelers to the bottom of her ballet slippers. "Can you be scary, but never scared?"

"Sometimes," said Daphne.

"Do you like lizard pancakes?" Chip asked.

"My favorite," she answered.

"Most important," I added, "can you laugh a scary laugh?"

Daphne took a deep breath. *"WOO-HOOO-AHH-HA-HA!"*

"Very good," I said, clapping.

Chip nodded. "Yes, she shows promise."

I took Daphne's magic wand from her bag. I tapped it on her head, one time, two times, three.

"We, the Ghoul Brothers," I proclaimed, "now dub thee an honorary Ghoul-in-Training."

Daphne bowed. Her feelers went *Boing-Boing*.

"I always thought the Ghoul Brothers needed

a sister," said Chip.

"Me, too," I said.

"Me, three!" said Daphne.

I took her hand. Then we picked up our bags and hurried home, where we ate candy bars and dreamed of lizard pancakes.

About the Author

Lee Wardlaw is not a ghoul, but while growing up she trick-or-treated as Peter Pan, Jeannie the Genie, a fortune teller, and the Queen ("Off with Her Head!") of Hearts.

A former elementary school teacher, Ms. Wardlaw now writes full-time for young readers. *101 Ways to Bug Your Parents* and *Bubblemania: A Kid's Book of Bubble Gum* are two of her fifteen books.

Ms. Wardlaw lives in Santa Barbara, California, where she enjoys eating potato chips and wiggling her nose at her husband.

More great books from Troll

Wish Magic
by Elizabeth Koehler-Pentacoff
illustrated by R. W. Alley

Teacher's Pest
by Candice Ransom
illustrated by Meredith Johnson

Goldfish Charlie and the Case of the Missing Planet
by Anne Mazer
illustrated by Jerry Harston

Available wherever you buy books.

Wish
Magic

by
Elizabeth
Koehler-Pentacoff

illustrated by
R. W. Alley

Meg doesn't suspect a thing when her weird brother, Morris, gives her a powdered doughnut one morning. But right after she eats the doughnut, strange things start happening. Meg realizes that the breakfast treat has given her special powers—everything she wishes for comes true! Wish magic can be lots of fun, but it also brings Meg all kinds of problems. Will she ever be a regular kid again?

ISBN 0-8617-3875-0

Available wherever you buy books.

Teacher's Pest

by
Candice Ransom

illustrated by
Meredith Johnson

Dudley loves his new teacher. But Miss Swallow isn't pleased by Dudley's funny antics and attention-getting schemes. Instead, she thinks nerdy R.J. is the perfect student. Miss Swallow even gives R.J. the lead in the Parents' Night class play—a part Dudley wanted for himself. Now Dudley is determined to steal the spotlight from R.J. on Parents' Night!

ISBN 0-8167-4017-8

Available wherever you buy books.

Goldfish Charlie
and the
Case of the
Missing Planet

by
Anne Mazer

illustrated by
Jerry Harston

No crime is too tough for Stray Cat Sam and Goldfish Charlie, the smartest and funniest detective team ever.

Someone has stolen a model of Planet Earth made by Charlie's owner. Sam and Charlie think a bully named Martin is the thief, but searching for the boy puts Sam in terrible danger.

Can Charlie save the planet before Sam uses up his nine lives?

ISBN 0-8167-4141-7

Available wherever you buy books.